Arthur Starter Book 05

ARTHUR
Tells a Story

by Marc Brown

Long tail Books

"Arthur, I'm bored," said D.W. "Tell me a story."
Arthur sighed. "Not now, D.W."
"Please?" she said.

"I can't," said Arthur. "I'm too busy."
"You don't look busy to me," said D.W.
"Well, I am," Arthur insisted. "I have to take Pal for a walk."
"Can I go, too?" D.W. asked.

"You could," said Arthur. "Except Pal and I are climbing a mountain today. A really, really steep one."

"I love climbing," D.W. said. "I'll get my sneakers!"

“No,” said Arthur. “It’s too dangerous.
There’s a volcano at the top of the mountain.
If it erupts, we’ll be blown across the ocean.”
“Sounds like fun!” said D.W.

"Not at all," Arthur told her. "When we finally land, we'll be in the jungle. There will be wild animals everywhere."

"Any unicorns?" asked D.W.

Arthur shook his head. "Anyway, after we escape from the jungle we'll have to swim back across the ocean. You can't swim."

"That's okay," said D.W. "I'll take a boat."

"But once we get on shore, there will be reporters and photographers everywhere," said Arthur.
"You might get trampled in the crowd."
"Or maybe I'll get to be on TV!" D.W. said.

"There won't be time," Arthur explained. "We'll have to go right to the White House. The President will want to meet us."

"Ooooh, the White House!" cried D.W.

"Sorry," said Arthur. "You have to be on a special list to get in. And you're not on it."

D.W. smiled. "I'm sure they'll let me in.
Wait till they see my new dress and party shoes!"

"It doesn't matter," said Arthur. "We're taking a helicopter home, and there's only room for Pal and me. Besides, we'll be in a hurry. We have to get here in time to lead the big hometown parade."

"Oh," said D.W.

"So now do you understand why I can't tell you a story?" asked Arthur.

"Yes," said D.W. "And thanks."

"Thanks?" Arthur frowned. "Thanks for what?"

D.W. smiled. “That was the best story ever!”